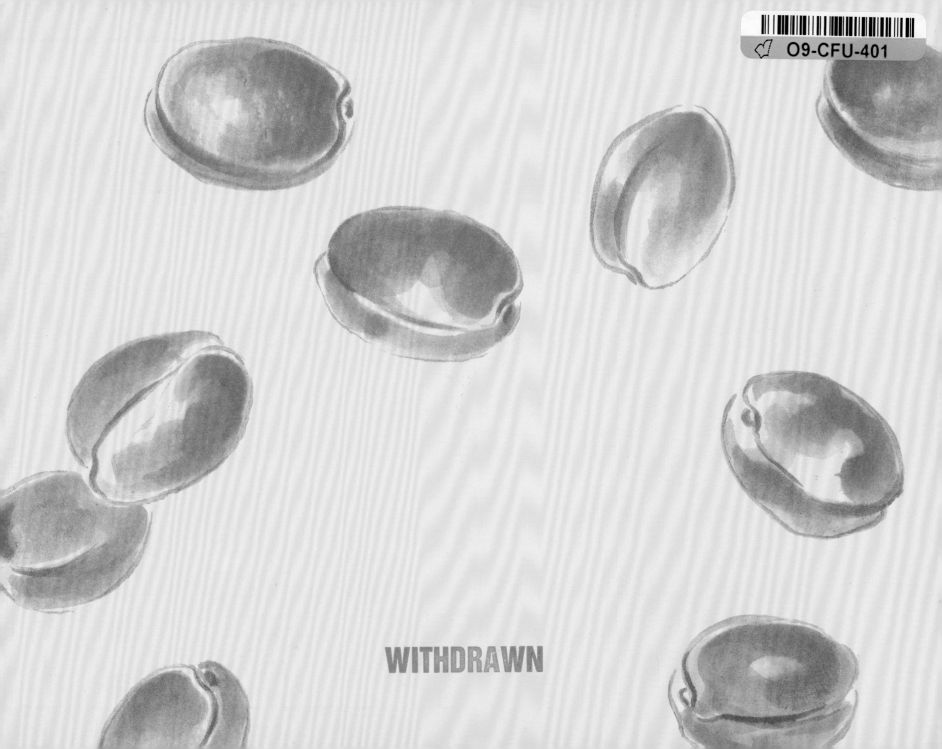

To the children of Afghanistan

The Most Beautiful Village in the World

Yutaka Kobayashi

Museyon, New York

Plums, cherries, pears, pistachios.
It's spring.
The village of Paghman is filled with flowers.

It's summer.

Every year, when the wind rustles the leaves,

and the fruits sway on the branches,

the people of the village go out and pick

plump apricots, plums, and cherries.

Harvest, when a sweet scent fills the air,

is the happiest time of the year.

" ♫ Are there plums? Are there pears?

Are there bright red beads of cherries?

Got them? Ate them?

Or died without eating them?"

Usually Yamo races with his brother Haroon to pick

plums and fill his basket.

But this summer Haroon is not here.

There is a war in Yamo's country.

And his brother is a soldier.

Today Yamo is going into town for the first time with Pompa, the donkey, to sell fruit. He is going to help his father in place of his brother.

"Good-bye, Mom!" Yamo leaves home early in the morning with his father.
The heavy baskets of sweet plums and bright red cherries are swaying on Pompa's back.

"Hey, Yamo. Are you going somewhere?" the people of the village call to him.

"Yep. I'm going with my dad."   "Okay. Hope you sell a lot!"

Along the way, Yamo repeats the words that his father has taught him:
"Cherries here! Sweet little suns! Cherries from Paghman!"

The sun rises over the road, and suddenly it's hot.

Buses and trucks heading to town pass Yamo and his father.

They arrive in town. Excited voices are everywhere. There is a sheep market.
A man selling roasted beans shouts loudly.

Yamo can smell shish kebab roasting and bread baking. There are also the smells
of carpets and books. The town is so lively that Yamo's heart beats faster.

Yamo's father finally decides to open his stand in
the large plaza where people go back and forth.
"I'm going to sell the plums here in this plaza.
Why don't you walk around town and try to sell
the cherries?"

"All by myself?"

"Pompa will be with you. He knows his way around this town."

He has no choice, so Yamo starts to walk. It's as if he's being pulled along by Pompa.

First Pompa takes Yamo to the covered bazaar.
Small, colorful shops are crammed side by side.

People are shopping. Some are drinking tea.

Can I sell my cherries in a place like this? Yamo worries.

He gathers his courage and shouts. "Cherries here!" No one turns around.

He tries shouting louder. "Cherries! Cherries from Paghman here!"

Yamo uses his small voice as he passes in front of fruit shops.   "Cherries. . . ."

RING! RING! RING! RING! "Watch out! Watch out! Get out of my way!"

A horse taxi races past Yamo, ringing its bells.

The town is so hectic, it makes Yamo dizzy. No one buys his cherries.
Disappointed, Yamo sits down by the roadside. Then . . .
"I want cherries from Paghman, please!" a little girl says.

After that, Yamo's cherries sell quickly.
"Little boy, will you give me some?
 I used to grow fruit near Paghman.
 Those were good years."
"Were you in the war, sir?"
"I was. That's where I lost my leg."
Yamo is shocked. He thinks about his brother Haroon.

The man puts a cherry into his mouth.
"Very sweet and a bit sour. Paghman's cherries
 are always so tasty. They're the best in the world!"

"Dad! I sold all my cherries!"

Yamo's father, standing behind his plums, smiles. He's sold fewer than half.

"Is that so! Then why don't we take a break and get something to eat?"
Yamo's father asks the man next to him to watch over his stand.

Yamo and his father eat their late lunch in a *chaikhana*, a teahouse. Good smells fill the air. Yamo tells his father what he saw in the town.

"A man who lost his leg in the war bought my cherries too. He said that Paghman's cherries are the best in the world." Yamo takes out a handful of cherries.

"I kept some because I wanted to eat them with you, Dad."

The man sitting next to them starts talking.
"You've sold a lot, haven't you?"
"My son Yamo did. My older son has gone to the war."
"That's worrisome. I've heard that the war in the south
  is quite hard."
"He says that he should be back by next spring."
  Yamo listens while he drinks sweet tea. He believes
  that his brother Haroon will be all right, but . . .
  Yamo worries.

  Just then his father whispers, "I have a surprise
  for you later, Yamo."
"What!? What is it? Tell me, please."
"We still have to sell the rest of the plums."
  Yamo puts the last cherry into his mouth. They say
  good-bye to the man and leave the tearoom.

The sound of prayer is heard from the mosque in the plaza.
A sense of serenity embraces the town.

"Plums! Plums here! Plums from Paghman!" Yamo calls while he thinks of what his father told him. *What could the surprise be?*

Finally, all the plums have been sold.

"Now we can go to where the surprise is."

Yamo's father walks straight across the plaza with him.

Yamo can't wait.

From on top of his father's shoulders, he sings loudly,

"♫ What is it? What is it?

What's the surprise?"

They come to the sheep market. Yamo's father buys a young lamb
with all the money they earned.

It is a pure white lamb. It will be the first sheep that Yamo's family has ever owned. No one else in their village has such a beautiful lamb.

"Now, Pompa, let's go home. Everyone is going to
be surprised to see this lamb."

Eventually they arrive in their village. It smells like home. Although Yamo has been away from the village for just one day, he feels like he has returned from a very long trip.

"Everyone is looking at our lamb."

Yamo walks along the village street with his chest puffed up.

Yamo asks his father if he can give the lamb a name. He calls it
Bahaar. The name means "spring."
"Please come home quick, Brother Haroon. We have a new member
of the family." Spring is still nearly a year away.

In the winter,
the village was destroyed in the war.

It no longer exists.

For those who would like to know more about the village of Paghman:

This story takes place in Afghanistan in South Asia.

It hardly rains in Afghanistan. People often think of the country as a land covered with dry soil, rocks, and sand because of the climate. However, the country has mountains with perpetual snow on top, forests, and vast grasslands that stretch as far as the eye can see. In spring, plants and flowers grow and bloom, and abundant fruit grows during the summer.

The country is blessed by nature.

People have lived in Afghanistan for a long time, raising animals and cultivating fields.

However, a war began in this peaceful country. Many young people left their villages in the countryside to join the war. The war has spread throughout the nation, and millions of people have left their ruined homeland and become refugees in other countries.

I visited Afghanistan in the summer of the tenth year after the war began.

During my trip, I visited a small village. The people were cheerful and lived their lives passionately. And they welcomed a traveler like me with generosity.

The village of Paghman in this story is modeled after the village I visited. There I met young children like Yamo, as well as honorable people like Yamo's father, and made friends with them. However, just like Paghman, the village was later bombed and ruined. I do not know what happened to the friends I made in that village.

There are many more villages just like it in Afghanistan.

I wish the civil war in Afghanistan would end quickly, and that peaceful times would return to all the villages in the country. Then those who escaped to other countries could come home. And then I wish I could see my old friends, and that their village could become, once again, the most beautiful village in the world.

—Yutaka Kobayashi

The Most Beautiful Village in the World

Sekaiichi Utsukushii Boku no Mura © 1995 Yutaka Kobayashi
All rights reserved.

Publisher's Cataloging-in-Publication Data

Names: Kobayashi, Yutaka, 1946- author. | Gharbi, Mariko Shii, translator. | Kaplan, Simone, editor.

Title: The most beautiful village in the world / Yutaka Kobayashi ; translation by Mariko Shii Gharbi ; English editing by Simone Kaplan.

Other titles: Sekaiichi utsukushii boku no mura. English

Description: New York : Museyon, [2018] | Series: Yamo's village series. | "Originally published in Japan in 2015 by Poplar Publishing Co., Ltd."--Title page verso. | Audience: Ages 5-7. |

Identifiers: ISBN: 9781940842257 | LCCN: 2017963793

Subjects: LCSH: Fathers and sons--Juvenile fiction. | Afghanistan--Juvenile fiction. | Children-- Afghanistan--Fiction. | Families--Juvenile fiction. | Villages--Afghanistan--Juvenile fiction. | Market towns--Afghanistan--Juvenile fiction. | Children and war--Afghanistan--Juvenile fiction. | War and society--Juvenile fiction. | CYAC: Fathers and sons--Fiction. | Afghanistan --Fiction. | Children--Afghanistan--Fiction. | Families--Fiction. | Villages--Fiction. | Children and war--Fiction. | War and society--Fiction. | LCGFT: Picture books. | BISAC: JUVENILE FICTION / People & Places / Asia.

Classification:
LCC: PZ49.31.K63 S4513 2018 | DDC: [E]--dc23

Published in the United States/Canada by:
Museyon Inc.
333 East 45th Street
New York, NY 10017

Museyon is a registered trademark.
Visit us online at www.museyon.com

Originally published in Japan in 1995 by POPLAR Publishing Co., Ltd.
English translation rights arranged with POPLAR Publishing Co., Ltd.

Printed in China

ISBN 978-1-940842-25-7